Level 1 is ideal for child[...]
some initial reading instru[...]
very simply, using a small [...]
repeated words.

D0386104

Special features:

tree

the animals

honey

Giraffe

6

7

Opening pages
introduce key
story words

Careful match between
story and pictures

Day time came.

"Giraffe's head is stuck in
that tree," the animals said.
"We must pull her out."

"Slurp. Slurp." Giraffe said.

Large,
clear type

17

Tinga Tinga Tales is inspired by
traditional animal stories from Africa
and the Tingatinga artwork of Tanzania

Educational Consultant: Geraldine Taylor
Book Banding Consultant: Kate Ruttle

Created by Claudia Lloyd
Text adapted by Jillian Powell
Illustrations from the TV animation produced
by Tiger Aspect Productions Limited and
Homeboyz Entertainment Kenya
Artwork supplied by Noah Mukono

A catalogue record for this book is available from the British Library

Published by Ladybird Books Ltd
80 Strand, London, WC2R 0RL
A Penguin Company

009

This edition MMXIII

ISBN: 978-0-72327-331-8

Printed in China

Why Giraffe Has a Long Neck

Based on a script by
Edward Gakuya
and Claudia Lloyd

the animals

tree

honey

Giraffe

7

There was a time when Giraffe did not have a long neck or long legs.

There was also a time when Giraffe had an upset tummy.

"Honey will help your upset tummy!" the animals said.

There was some honey in the tree. So Giraffe popped her head in the tree.

"Slurp! I love honey!" Giraffe said.

Then Giraffe said,
"I will pull my head out
of the tree now. Oh help!
I am stuck!"

13

"I can't get my head out," Giraffe said. "I am stuck!"

Night time came.

"Slurp. I love honey," Giraffe said.

Day time came.

"Giraffe's head is stuck in that tree," the animals said. "We must pull her out."

"Slurp. Slurp." Giraffe said.

17

So the animals pulled
Giraffe's legs.

"You must not
get upset. We will
get your head out,"
the animals said.

A long time went by.

"Now we will also
pull the tree!"
the animals said.

21

So all the animals
pulled and pulled...

Then the animals said,
"Oh no! Look how long
Giraffe's neck has got!"

23

More days and nights went by. The tree got taller and taller.

"Look how long Giraffe's neck has got now!" said the animals.

"Giraffe, we can't pull your head now. YOU must pull it," the animals said. "Pull!" Giraffe's head popped out.

"I did it! I am out of the tree!" said Giraffe.

And that is why
Giraffe has a long neck!

How much do you remember about the story of Tinga Tinga Tales: Why Giraffe Has a Long Neck? Answer these questions and find out!

- What food does Giraffe slurp?

- Where is Giraffe's head stuck?

- Which animals help get Giraffe out of the tree?